# A THORNE IN TIME

An Eva Thorne series prequel novella

Lorel Clayton

LC Books
Sydney

A Thorne in Time/ Lorel Clayton. -- 1st ed.
ISBN 978-0-9942290-6-9

*We choose our future, not our past.*

—Hazel

# 1   GOODBYES

I hated the red, which came out looking like rust rather than the blood I was going for. I washed hair dye from my hands and stained a good towel cleaning up. I didn't need a mirror to know the new shade made me unnaturally pale.

"I am unnatural," I told my reflection.

I shoved clothes into my bags. Punched them in more like. It felt good to vent. Morgan would chastise me for not folding anything, but he wouldn't be coming. He'd never know what a wreck I made of things.

"Get up you lazy, pathetic excuse for a Thorne!" Nanny's screech carried through the house. I wouldn't miss that. I didn't know if she was talking about me or

Ilsa, probably me, as the Dark One she avoided with superstitious dread. "Eva!" So, she did mean me.

"I'm coming," I screeched back. I added an elvish brassiere to my suitcase—wishful thinking, as I was thirteen and still flat as a board, but I might 'bloom' soon as Karo put it—and dashed out the door and down the stairs to the entry hall.

The suitcase was new, the type with wheels that could move about on their own if there was magic to fuel it. Of course, no one had bought any of the green goo to run it, so it was extra heavy with dormant motors. Useless thing. I hefted it in two hands and tossed it at Morgan, proud of my athleticism. He was twice my height and built of muscle, so he hardly noticed the extra weight.

"I'm not leaving yet. I'll meet you at the gate." I tossed the knapsack at him too, along with the other bag I'd dragged down the steps behind me.

"Eva?" He raised an eyebrow, but Morgan was good. Not 'good' in the sense he never hurt a fly, as he hurt more than a few of them being the house steward, and he also hurt more than flies, being my uncle's bodyguard. He was 'good' in that he would trust me and not tattle to Uncle Ulric. Nanny on the other hand....

"Where are you off to?" Her voice hadn't lowered a decibel. I stuck my fingers in my ears, but she didn't get the hint, not even when Morgan dropped all the bags on the marble floor and stoppered his ears too.

"You have an education to get, little missy," she continued. "Learn to be a proper lady, leave the nest, stop being a burden upon your poor uncle and me with all your constant complaints, your judging and sniping. Wish it were a proper Solhan school; they'd teach you a lesson." Solhan schools were the kind where three out of ten students survived, so it could be worse. Barely.

"I don't want to be a lady!" I dashed out the front door before Uncle came to investigate the commotion.

I didn't want to leave Highcrowne, but I knew when I'd lost. With Uncle, the only option was losing. One silent look from him and I froze. He didn't need a bodyguard like Morgan when he had a look like that.

There was one person I had to see before I went away. Okay, two, and they were always together.

My boots skittered over icy stones, and I slipped in a few spots, going with it, letting my feet glide a bit before I regained my balance and picked them up again. It was sort of a running skate action as I made my way across the Outskirts.

We lived in the best section of the dung heap, but it was still a dung heap. Literally. Piles of horse manure, human and other offal were shoved into the corners or waiting in the middle of the road for you to step in, or for the goblin street cleaners to come, but it usually got stepped in before they showed.

No one cared about refugees like us. Bad as Uncle was, he and other members of the local council had built a civilization out of nothing—real houses and temples, businesses and schools, although none good enough for a Thorne—with no help from the kings who ruled the city. Our monarchs were dwarf, elf, and Avian, so why would they care about humans? Forget about Solhans, like me. We were the most unnatural. The failures of the world. The worst of the worst. This is what happened when a great culture fell: it fell hard.

When I reached the outskirts of the Outskirts is when it got really depressing. This was where the most desperate refugees lived, those newly come to the city without patron or family or anyone to help them. No cobbles, no stone buildings. It was all mud and filth and shacks made of discarded wood, if the people were lucky, straw and tarpaulins of oil-treated cloth if they weren't. It wasn't enough to keep out Highcrowne winter, and the frozen dead were found covered in whatever rags their families could spare. They didn't lay in the street long at least. Someone came by to burn them every morning. Leaving them would have been a very, very bad idea.

The Crowns cared about hazards to the city proper, if not the people who huddled at the city's feet begging for help and mercy from the horrors of the world outside. I hadn't encountered those horrors, heard about them only. But if what I saw here was any indication, if this was the place of solace for people, how much worse must it be beyond the borders of the Three Kingdoms?

For some reason, my brother, Uncle's heir and favored one, chose to come here every day. I did too, to be with him and, you know—Duane.

Duane stood, back against a wall, doing nothing, and he looked great doing it. He was next to a burning brazier, but he wasn't huddled around it like the family beside him or the people on the other side of the square who crowded around their own small fires. They all shivered and rubbed their hands to stay warm, while he radiated heat of his own. He wasn't even wearing a jacket. Maybe he didn't own one, but it didn't matter. He looked hot. I mean in terms of 'not cold'. Not cold at all.

"Hey there, Eva." Somehow, I'd blinked and he was standing beside me. He was fast, but I think I lost time around him. I needed to sleep more, as he often sent me into a daydream.

"Hi," I squeaked.

"So, you're headed out of this filth hole today. Lucky you. You lookin' for Vikky?"

"Yes," I managed through a throat that had swollen up.

"He's over at the market grabbing some grain. You know. I'm here to distribute, while he hides out for a bit. All part of the plan. You up for helping with the plan?"

"Yeah, sure." I always agreed to whatever he asked. It was automatic. "But, I gotta get going. Coach is heading out. I'll go find him. Only. You got a minute?"

"What you need?"

"Um. In private. Over there." I pointed to what amounted to an alley between two shanties, one made of broken crates and tumbled stones stolen from the wall, and the other of tarpaulin, tied to a wood frame using cat gut. Lots and lots of cat gut. The rest of the cats were probably eaten and the bones turned into forks, what with how thorough refugees could be about using what they had. Poor kitties; in the wrong neighborhood at the wrong time. I'd been eyeing the secluded and relatively clean spot and led the way, Duane following, quiet as usual.

He never spoke unless he had something to say. I liked that about him. It was a bit unnerving, though, when the two of us were standing there. I couldn't look at him. His face anyway. I saw his dirty hands dangling next to filthier breeches and a shirt that should have been white but was brown and gray. He was thin but starting to grow muscle faster than I was growing a chest. I felt awkward standing next to him.

"Duane?"

"Yes?"

"I'm going to be gone for years. Years. I'll...I'll miss you. Will you miss me?"

"It's a long time."

"Don't forget about me." I looked up then, into his green eyes, and my heart was fluttering so madly I thought I'd throw up.

I grabbed the back of his neck with a sweaty palm. He was older and taller than me, so I practically had to climb him to reach, but I gave him a kiss. On the lips!

There were running footsteps then, and my brother shouted, "Hey!"

Duane backed away so fast I thought his feet were on fire. He wiped his lips with the back of his hand and gave me a surprised look. And that was it.

He ran out to the square where Viktor handed him a bag of grain. Duane did a circuit of the square with the heavy bag on his shoulder, spilling out piles in every shanty house he passed, with cheers and pats from the locals. He got all the credit for Viktor's risk.

Duane shot me a look every once in a while, an expression I could only call dismay. Or horror. I should never have kissed him. Not ever.

"This is a good hiding spot." Viktor was checking out the alley where I stood, rooted. "I'll stay here for a while, in case the guards come. I was pretty fast. Not sure they even saw me."

"Why didn't you buy the grain?" I said, annoyed. I adored my big brother; he could do no wrong, but the stunts he pulled with Duane made me doubt his wisdom.

"Uncle counts every coin. I can't steal from him, and with what little he gives me, he expects me to buy certain clothes, certain arms, certain everything. If I'm not wearing them, he notices. So much effort spent on pretense rather than dealing with reality, but that's our family, isn't it? Our worth should be based on actions, not appearances, and most people's actions are lacking. Helping people means I need to be willing to put my neck on the line. It means more this way."

I didn't know what to say, so I gave him a hug.

"What's that for?"

"I'm going. Today."

"That's today?" He ran his hands through his black hair, a black so pure it was darker than night. My hair was that color when I didn't dye it. "Uncle is going to kill me for not seeing everyone off." He kicked the poorly mortared wall, and it jiggled a bit.

"Don't worry. Uncle didn't see anyone off either. At least I don't think so. I left while Morgan was still packing the carriage. You didn't want to say goodbye to Ilsa did you?"

He smiled. "Yeah, I did. She's my favorite sister, don't you know?"

I punched him. "Well, you're stuck saying goodbye to this one."

"At least you look the same." He shrugged and gave me another hug. It turned into a real one once my stiff anger faded. "I love you, Eva."

"Love you too."

It was hard letting him go, but I knew I was late. It was time to get on with my life. At least start dealing with what it threw at me. I waved as I ran off, and he peeked out of hiding to give me one last wave too.

The guards weren't coming. They didn't care about the Outskirts. The only ones who policed these streets were my uncle's cronies, and they wouldn't say anything. I spotted a few of them in shadows, sneering at Duane and Viktor. 'Do-gooder', they called my brother, like that was a bad thing. The worst of them, the one they called Gas, gave me a tip of the hat as I went past. He was only a few years older than Viktor but had a worldliness in his eyes I never liked, a hell of experience trapped behind black pupils, and it always looked like he wanted to share that hell with me. He gave me the creeps. I gave him a rude gesture and kept going.

Through informants like Gas, Uncle knew all about Viktor's antics. There was no rebelling. Uncle allowed it for some reason. I don't know why Viktor hadn't figured that out yet. Maybe he needed to believe he was a rebel? I certainly wasn't. I was cowed and doing exactly what Uncle wanted. I'd soon be miles away from him and Ilsa. It couldn't come soon enough.

# 2   Far from Here

"What's she doing here?" I asked when I reached the motor carriage waiting for me by the Outskirts' gate.

It was an unnatural sort of carriage, shuddering and chattering, and moved slower than horses could pull it, but it was expensive, imported from the Fortress of Mages in the South, and Uncle was showing off by owning it. I thought it would break down before we got more than a few feet away from the gate. It wasn't a real gate like the city had, more a symbolic one sectioning off the richer section of refugees from the poorer section. Still, it was easier for Morgan to meet me there than get stuck in the mud of the shanty town.

The 'she' I was referring to was my twin sister, Ilsa. She was looking at me with those creepy white eyes of hers. Mine were enchanted blue, so I could pretend for a moment we weren't identical. Her black hair was plaited in the most elaborate style I'd yet seen, woven into a bird's nest atop her head, with birds in it. Or was it bats? That's where she'd been all morning, surely. Getting her hair done.

"We're taking her to the docks first." Morgan was in the front seat, my baggage crammed next to him, while Ilsa's luggage filled the storage trunk at the back and was hanging out, tied down with rope. That left the rear seat for Ilsa and me to share. Great.

"Get in," Ilsa told me. "I don't want to be late."

"We will be if we ride in this. Come on, Morgan. I thought you were ready to leave this thing in the junk heap last week. What about One-sy? Doesn't she want to get out of the stable now and then?" One-sy had lost an eye years ago, and she was more a pet than a horse. "She could go faster than this thing."

Morgan cocked his head and glanced back at Ilsa, decked out in furs and sparkling jewelry. That said it all. This had been her idea. She wanted to look important.

"Fine." I liked how my twin curled her lip and her legs away from my dirty boots as I climbed in. There was a blanket on the seat, which she didn't need with all those furs. I yanked it away before she could react and tossed it out into the street. Someone grabbed it before it got wet.

"Eva," she growled.

I ignored her and rooted around in my bags, leaning over the seat and winking at Morgan. He rolled his eyes, used to our squabbles. I dug out a few things and shifted others around until I had a knapsack stuffed with clothes, mostly sweaters and warm things. I could always buy more in Gernwold.

"I've decided not to bring this stuff." I threw the bag through the shanty gate. I didn't see who got what, as so many people pulled at it, but I felt better knowing someone might not freeze tonight. I eyed Ilsa's boxes.

"Get moving, now," she snapped. Morgan obeyed, and the carriage trundled forward. I sat down with a disappointed exhale.

"You won't even need furs in Faellion," I told her.

"You know nothing about it. I will be in the best school in the Three Kingdoms, where the elven royals are tutored."

"Distant royals," I muttered.

"There could be trips to the highlands, weekends by the sea. The wind could get blustery."

"They have palm trees."

I didn't know why she got Faellion, with its famed, pink crystal towers, while I got Gernwold. I'd never been to the Dwarf Lands, but I heard it was more of the same I'd known all my life: snow, mountains, ice...more snow. The Elf Lands might have been nice, if not for the elves. But as long as Ilsa and I were a kingdom away from each other, I'd be happy, which was the real reason I willed the carriage to go faster.

We had blissful silence all the way to the docks. It took so long to unload Ilsa's things and cart them to the ship, I thought we might be late to meet the stagecoach. I thrilled at that. A week longer at home, and a week late for school, before the next one came. Sounded like a plan.

There were no hugs or false goodbyes. Ilsa didn't wave or look back before she boarded the ship.

I gauged the sun. We were still on time. Damn. The motor carriage didn't die going up the steep path from the docks, either. It actually made better time than the mules and donkeys we passed. Damn, again. The carriage kept up its relentless pace all the way across the massive bridge that overlooked the Serpent's Ribbon, and I thought I spotted Ilsa's ship below.

"Don't lean out so far," Morgan said. I obeyed, feeling slightly woozy from the height anyway.

The carriage made better time on the straightaway, and before I knew it we were at the stables. The horses were restless and danced about, the groomsmen trying to keep them calm. I thought it was our carriage riling them up and told Morgan to turn the motor off, but then I heard the noises that were annoying them: Distant hammering and booming, a hissing clank accompanying each bang.

"Steam machines," Morgan explained. "For the rail line."

"What's that?"

"Something to replace the stagecoach to Gernwold."

"Let's wait for it."

"It's not built yet."

"I can wait."

He did the eyebrow thing again, and I sighed. He handed my bags to the coach driver who packed them away. It was full and would leave soon. Time to go.

I couldn't do it. "Morgan..." I began. He gave me a hug, and I cried then. Just a little. I wiped my eyes before he could see. He was Solhan, believe it or not, but even as different as he was from Nanny and Uncle, he would chide me for weeping. Thornes could not be weak.

My eyes were dry again by the time I pulled away and climbed into the coach. Karo had saved a seat for me. Unfortunately, it was opposite Juliette.

I sat and glared at Juliette for a moment. She glared back. She wasn't Solhan, so it wasn't as effective, blunted by her blonde hair and cornflower blue eyes. She backed down first, turning to gaze out a window with her nose in the air.

"What's with you two?" Karolyne asked. "Every time you meet it's a contest of wills. You must have some reason to hate her so?"

"No reason. We've never spoken. I just don't like her." Being friends with Ilsa told me all I needed to know. Juliette could hear me but pretended not to.

"You've gone red, like me," Karolyne said, finally noticing my terrible dye job. "We look like sisters!" Hardly, but I let her be thrilled.

"She still looks Solhan to me." Juliette used Solhan as an expletive. Did she forget Ilsa was too? Ilsa had a way of making people forget, of course, of charming anyone she wanted. I'd seen her lies in action before and been amazed. My sister never showed me that side, so I always marveled at how easily-fooled people were. It was my turn to ignore Juliette.

"Glad you're here to keep me company," I told Karo. Her father paid tribute to my uncle, the lines on Saturday often long to see him, so all us children had played together. We were old friends. "This trip will go by in no time."

I was being facetious. It was, of course, long and horrible.

Ten days over bumpy mountain roads, stopping in dodgy inns to eat or rest, our group of soon-to-be-ladies clustered together for protection from the locals.

We were in dwarf lands, so there were lots of lonely men. Very lonely men, as there was a dozen for every female. The coach driver had to use his whip to keep them at bay at one point. Not that they were danger-ous or impolite. They all had flowers and gifts on offer, and they deferred to the women matriarchs who ruled them, but unattached females were such a rare sight in those towns we caused quite a furor.

It was a relief when we arrived in Gernwold. Not a relief from the cold, however. If anything, it was colder than the depths of winter in Highcrowne, which was hard to imagine. Perhaps it was the lack of warm bodies all pressed together, or the vast squares of stone monuments, stone benches and even stone carriages that made the place colder than it should be.

We were on an artificial plateau, cut from the side of the mountain, so it was strange to encounter such a flat city when jagged mountains loomed all around. It was too cold for fresh snow. What there was had been trampled into the stone streets or clung to shadowy corners away from the stomp of sturdy, dwarvish feet. Everything was hard and ancient and unyielding, like the dwarf who opened the carriage door, jammed suitcases into our hands and left us to find our own way. The coachman pointed at a castle-like structure within the castle that was the city, and that was all we had to navigate by.

It wasn't as grand a city as Highcrowne, no ornate gates, exotic wares and tradesmen from foreign lands, but it lacked anything like the Outskirts, so it was a lot cleaner. It was somewhat cosmopolitan, with a few humans, elves and goblins about, but it was predominantly dwarf. I thought there were a lot of dwarves in Highcrowne, but here they teemed.

Dwarves manned the cranes unloading huge, horse-drawn trucks full of ore that carried the tang of rust and the acridness of sulfur. Cargos of ore were replaced by food and steel tools bound for the famous mines that riddled the mountains. Huge forges with bellows as tall as a house wheezed and clanked, the dwarf smiths turning ore into tools in an endless cycle. The food stalls we passed smelled of earth and mold, when were lucky, manure when we were unfortunate to get a whiff, as the odor clung to clothes and lingered in nostrils some time afterward.

Mushrooms of every type, size and color were on offer, one advertised as 'nutty' and another 'as sweet as your dear mum's smile'. With so little arable land but so much cavernous space below ground, mushrooms were the prime food supply, that and sightless cattle who dwelled in darkness all their lives. I'd read about it in a story called 'The Mystery of the Missing Cow' where it turned out a cave troll had moved in to harass a dwarf farmer, but he was under the employ of a rival House, so there was a lot more to it than a hungry troll. The grall natives got involved too, angered by incursions into their native territory.

That was the extent of my dwarvish knowledge, really: books and the occasional merchant my uncle might have dealings with. Dwarves outnumbered everyone in Highcrowne, but there was a separation between them and us—and between elves and everyone else, of course—all in our own sections, overlapping at trade or work in the day, but all nicely categorized in our beds come nightfall. Now, I would be living among dwarves every day and every night, and I didn't know the first thing about them. Not really.

I did know their seats were uncomfortable. I sat on a stone bench while the other girls from the coach stopped to browse the market, and it felt like my bum was being frozen, turned into stone as well. Were dwarf bums somehow immune to cold? The seat was too short, my knees in my face, so I decided to sit on my suitcase instead.

I hated mushrooms, so I was hoping to spot something else edible on the food stalls. Uncle promised to send me a stipend every few months. I'd have to stock up on those swamp melons imported from the goblin lands, which smelled of honey. I wished I could buy some of the sweet tubers trucked in from elvish farms, but the teachers probably wouldn't let me roast them in my room. Such imported foods were expensive, though, so it would have to be blind beef most of the time.

"You could try a mushroom for once." Karolyne giggled when she waved the bag beneath my nose and I retched.

"I'm not eating anything that grows in manure and rot and is half animal. It's strange." I felt I was stating the obvious.

"Everything grows in manure and rot, even animals," she countered.

"It's the half animal, half plant nature of mushrooms that frightens me. How can I be sure it's dead before I eat it? I'm not into live food."

"Did you see that?" Karo wasn't listening to me by now. She pointed to a small dwarf figure—they were all small, of course, which made it easier for someone lanky and long-legged like me to see over their heads and take in everything—who was wearing a head-to-toe golden veil. It looked to be constructed of gold threads woven together and encrusted with the odd diamond or other gem. "A tidy fortune walking around there."

"It's a Matriarch. One of the ruling class of dwarves. There are a few other dwarf women about too."

Most women had swarms of children clustered around them begging for treats from the market. They looked a lot like the men, only beardless, for the most part, and with far more striking eyes. All dwarfs had plain, muddy-looking skin and hair, but their eyes were like gems plucked from the mountains: sapphire, polished ocher, topaz.... The females' versions glowed with inner light. I wondered if a Matriarch's eyes were different still?

"How do you know about Matriarchs?"

I sat straighter and tried to sound superior. "I read."

"You mean all those trash mysteries and romances and the like?"

I glared. She was my only friend, so I put up with it, but sometimes....

The migration of school girls organically moved on, and we eventually reached a tall building with spires and turrets, where we hoped the school was. It looked closer when we started out, but the press of dwarfs made navigation difficult and slow, not to mention all the luggage we dragged around, and the stopping to browse. It was a defense mechanism against all the strangeness around us. Shopping was familiar and comforting, when we all felt extremely uncomfortable. Our gaggle of six human girls towered over everyone and drew more stares than the Matriarch did.

We finally reached the gates and were waved through by dwarves in the school colors of maroon and steel: Maroon tabards and steel weapons. Looked like they needed to display a bit of force to keep the ladies safe, and it worked, as the crowds outside kept a wide berth.

Juliette was gasping, as though our walk had been a marathon. When she regained her breath, she waved a kerchief at the guards. "I hope our uniforms are not the same dreadful shade. No one looks good in maroon."

It was the shade I'd been going for when I dyed my hair. I couldn't help saying, "Don't you know anything? Of course our uniforms will be the same color."

Oh, no. I'd spoken to her directly. That put a target on my chest, which I realized the moment she smiled, cat-like.

"What I do know is that Solhans are no more welcome here than they are anywhere else."

I was about to say something clever, biting and unforgettable, at least pretty sure it would have been good, when a commotion outside the school gate drew my attention. A dark-haired Solhan girl pounded on the bars until the guards let her through. She was dressed in maroon, the school crest on her gloves and cloak.

"Wonderful. Another one. Father should ask for my tuition back and send me someplace respectable, like Faellion, or Archon in the south, where you can find real humans." Juliette huffed and walked inside.

I went to the Solhan, same white skin as me, and touched her trembling shoulder. She jumped.

"It's okay," I said.

When she looked at me, I realized she must be only half-Solhan, for her features were clearly elf: large, almond eyes, sharp chin and cheekbones, and the points of ears peeking out of her limp hair. Half-elven anything was a rarity to see. Let alone Solhan. We were the despised.

"What happened? What are you frightened of?" I didn't mean to interrogate her, but the questions, instead of rattling her more, calmed her.

She said, "Thank you."

"I didn't do anything."

"You touched me. Most people are afraid the taint is catching. My family sent me here, across the kingdoms, so they'd never have to see me or touch me again."

I felt a pang for her. I knew what it was like to be different from everyone around you. "Why were you running just now?"

"Someone was following me. They're gone now. Never mind. I get...confused. See things that aren't really there. I try to ignore them, as everyone says it's in my mind, but it's hard sometimes."

"What's your name?"

"Hazel."

"I'm Eva...Thorne." I hesitated to say my last name, as it marked me, like her half-breed 'taint' marked her. Everyone knew who my uncle was. Hazel didn't blink, though, and I realized then I was not in Highcrowne anymore. No one knew my family. I could be anybody.

"It's good to meet you," I said. "Can you show me around?"

She nodded and her eyes widened, either from amazement at my unexpected friendliness or because of something else terrifying only she could see. I wasn't frightened off by her; it was the odd people who tended to draw me in, as they were so much more interesting than everyone else.

A matron arrived to bark orders, and we all went inside, still dragging our own luggage across the bumpy cobbles. We were assigned rooms, me with Karo at least, but it got busy and the elf girl wandered away quietly before giving me a tour. I'd have to find her later.

I tossed my things into the stone chest beside my stone bed and sat down with a sigh. There was a mattress on the stone at least. Karolyne began carefully unpacking and sorting her garments. I hadn't opened my bags. The chest, more like a sarcophagus, was big enough to hold them all.

"I think I'm going to like it here." I leaned back on my pillow. Even sitting up, my feet hung off the edge of the bed. It was dwarf length.

"Because there are Solhans, or because we're taller than everyone?" Karo asked.

A glared at her. "No. Because it's not Highcrowne. I could tell people I'm a lost Darrub princess."

"No one would believe it."

"Let me dream a little."

"We're not here to dream. We're here to learn how to dance, sing, serve tea, and be generally appealing to men, so we can get married to a rich one and live happily ever after."

I glared some more. "This school was originally built to educate Matriarchs. There's classes on language, diplomacy, governorship...."

"You think they'll let a human into those classes? Oh, right, I've got to stop deflating your dreams. Go, sign up. Have fun."

I put the pillow over my head and curled into a fetal position to fit on the small mattress. I was so tired and so glad to be off that bumpy stagecoach I think I fell asleep. Not for long, as someone slapped the back of my hand, and I was up like a shot, ready to fight.

Ilsa and I had had a few fights in the early years before we turned to not speaking to one another. I was ready to have at her, or whoever—I was a bit groggy—but then I noticed it was a teacher. She wore the floppy hat and velvet mantle, but I didn't think the riding crop she carried around was regulation. Then again, had I read anything about school disciplinary policy? I couldn't remember. My hand was red and stinging.

"What was that for?" I left off the names I wanted to call her.

Morgan and Nanny had warned me many times in the last weeks to behave myself at school. 'Stay low and your time will go faster,' Morgan had advised, like it was prison, and Nanny had said, 'Please speak to them as you speak to us, and they'll whip you so quick you'll think I charmed you into horse form.' Whenever Nanny said 'please' you had to worry, and I didn't know if she could do a charm like that, but I suspected she could. Evidently, she'd known about the whip.

"You girls were expected yesterday." The teacher's ruby eyes had a fiery light I found disturbing. I wanted to explain about the coach's broken axle, which had been the main delay, but she didn't give me a chance to speak. "No lazing about now, ladies. If you can call yourselves that yet. Unkempt, clothes rumpled...." Karo was immaculate, but the teacher was looking at me. "Time for deportment lessons in the auditorium. Go. Don't keep everyone waiting any longer."

"Yes, Missus...?" Karolyne was such a kiss up.

"Madam Hale if you please, Miss Frost. Do remember that all dwarf women are Miss or Madam, unless they are a Lady, Baroness, Duchess or...not that you'll ever be gracious enough to meet one...a Matriarch. We have too many husbands to be anyone's 'missus', although you savage humans readily apply the term to any grown woman, in the assumption we all share your ways. You are in Gernwold now, and if your mothers had not begged and bribed your way into this school, you would not be here."

"I don't have a mother," I said for some reason.

"I know exactly how you gained entry, Miss Thorne." She tsked in a way that made it clear she did not approve, before turning on her heel and marching out, expecting us to follow.

Karolyne jumped to immediately, but I hesitated. I didn't think I was going to like it here after all.

None of the other girls in the auditorium looked very happy either, and not because we were late. It seemed a dour expression was required for deportment.

What kept throwing me off, as we waited in line for our chance to balance a book on our heads, was a mud-colored dwarf girl who kept smiling and waving at me. I looked behind me, but there was no one. I was the end of the line.

I waved back and got my hand slapped again. Was Madam Hale only watching me? The dwarf girl winced in sympathy. After class, which went on an interminable time—how much walking around with a straight spine can you manage without getting bored—the girl sought me out.

"Hi there."

"Do I know you?" I asked, puzzled.

"No, of course not. But I've seen your photograph. You recall having it taken when you applied?"

"My uncle applied for me." I remembered Morgan dragging me to the photography parlor. I should have realized something was up.

"Well, I've been assigned to be your orientation buddy. Welcome! I've been here two years and love it. Simply love it. Ask me anything?"

"You're still taking deportment two years in?"

"Yes, indeed. My favorite class. How hard is it to walk around for an hour? To sit and stand? I wish they were all like this."

"It gets worse?"

"You bet. Diplomacy, *ugh*. Elvish poetry, double *ugh ugh*. The only class better is fencing."

"Oh, please sign me up to that!" I said, excited by the thought of showing Madam Hale my foil next time she showed me her whip.

"Not sure they allow foreigners arms. I'll check. It would be great if we could have all our classes together. I could tell you everything about everything. I'm Gypsum, by the way."

"Eva."

"I knew that, silly. And you're Solhan. How amazing. Tell me all about it."

"What's to tell? We brought on the end of the world, ran for our lives, and now we live wherever we can. I live in Highcrowne. The Outskirts anyway."

"I want to live there!" Gypsum didn't seem to know anything but excited.

"I don't think you'd like the Outskirts."

"No, silly. Highcrowne. The Central City. The Matriarchs live there and help rule all the Kingdoms. I want to be one so much, but my older sister gets the title. She's a Baroness. While me, a mere decade younger, get nothing. Nada. Madam Gypsum for me. A few husbands lined up, the expected hordes of children. No, thank you."

"What can you do about it? Kill her to get the title?" It's what a Solhan would do, so it occurred to me right away. She looked shocked.

"I could never kill my own sister. No, there are other ways to get a title. Marriage for example, if you're human. If you're dwarf, there is pleasing your husband's Matriarch, and if she has no daughters.... Well, there's lots of opportunity for those willing to work for it. Come along now. We have sewing next. I'll show you where to get the best patterns."

Sewing? Ugh. Or as the dwarf girl said, double *ugh*. I asked if Gypsum had set my class schedule, but it was already assigned to me, and she was taking time away from some of her usual classes to show me around. Karolyne had an orientation buddy too, another dwarf who lacked Gypsum's enthusiasm for things. Karo drifted closer to us to be in on all the excitement.

"This is Karolyne," I told Gypsum, letting them strike up a conversation. They hit it off right away, for which I was glad. Gypsum's heart seemed to be in the right place, but I couldn't care less about what we were studying. At lunch, I left Gypsum and Karo chatting, while I slipped away to the library. I hoped it had books on something interesting.

By the time I found the place, lunch was nearly over, so I had little time to search. I had no idea how the shelves were organized. They were stone, of course, and elaborately carved, like everything in Gernwold. Only, instead of the standard scrollwork and decorative knots, these had symbols of fish, wolves and other creatures that somehow meant something to whoever organized the place. The library was a lot smaller than I hoped and had a disproportionate number of cookbooks, which in dwarvish cuisine amounted to many different ways of boiling or barbecuing everything to death.

Why did matriarchs need to know how to cook and sew? Didn't they have servants? I was beginning to suspect sexism was rampant among all races—women might rule in the dwarf lands, but they had to do everything else too.

I finally spotted an interesting section on history. Marginally interesting. But when the options were broiled blind-cow recipes versus the geopolitical origins of the Three Kingdoms, there was no point being choosy.

I went around a corner and ran into the half-Solhan girl I'd seen at the gate. I jumped, startled, as she'd been hiding. She put a finger to her lips, and said, "Someone's here."

I looked around frantically for an attacker. Morgan had trained me from a young age to be paranoid of kidnappers, brigands and other potential nasties in my environment. Of course, he hadn't planned for me to spend all day hanging out with thieves, like Duane, but I found they were easier to watch when you knew where to find them, and in Duane's case, much nicer to watch than other things.

Now, I wouldn't see him for months, not until I went home for break—if I could show my face to him again. I felt so humiliated. I had thought about 'the kiss' the whole coach ride over and realized I'd gone about it all wrong. My first half day of lessons had confirmed: I should have dressed up, baked some cookies...that was ridiculous too. I had no idea what I should have done, but I knew it hadn't been the best way, and now I'd blown it. I'd have to pretend it never happened.

Duane had me daydreaming again, even when he wasn't here. I shook off the fogginess and told the girl, "I don't see anyone. The library is deserted except for you and me."

"Good." She stayed crouched behind the stacks, shaking, with tears welling up in her eyes. I sat next to her and patted her on the shoulder.

"It's ok. What's really wrong?"

Hazel was different from any elf I'd met, or Solhan for that matter. An odd combination of the two. Usually, I couldn't stand elves, as all they did was complain, ridicule everyone and smell. Really bad. They didn't believe in bathing. They thought so highly of themselves they were convinced their natural odor smelled good. Their offal too. She had inherited the Solhan desire to be clean at least, but she lacked the killer fight over flight instinct of my race. Nanny or Morgan would have given her a lecture to really make her tremble, but I wasn't them. I tried to be patient and wait.

"Everyone hates me," she said.

"I don't."

"You don't know me."

"Then tell me more. I swear, unless you like to torture and reanimate house mice like my sister, I won't find anything to hate."

"I'm not a pure elf. I'm...Solhan."

She meant to shock me, but I'd already figured that one out. I said as much then added, "Me too."

"What? No. Your hair, your eyes...?"

"All a disguise. I know how it feels to be judged on sight. I also know lots of old Solhan stories Nanny shared, how sometimes Solhans see what no one else can. You're not crazy. Believe your eyes. And if there are any daemons or dark spirits lurking about, tell me where to go to steer clear." I smiled.

She nodded and wiped the tears from her face.

"Enough talk about the curses of being Solhan," I said. "I wanted to know more about you, not your ancestry. What do you like to do?"

"Read."

"Me too. What else?"

"I like embroidery class."

"You're losing me there. I cannot be friends with anyone who likes embroidery."

Her eyes started to tear up again, and I realized she was one of those poor souls with no sense of humor and probably no appreciation for sarcasm either. I'd have to be gentle with her.

"Only teasing. I want to be your friend anyway. What kind of books do you like?"

She grew visibly more comfortable as she talked about her favorite stories. I was aware I was late for whatever class I had next, and it didn't bother me, but she suddenly stopped mid-sentence. "I'm missing embroidery!" She grabbed her books and headed for the door.

"See you around," I called after.

She stopped and smiled shyly before she left.

I felt better, having met someone tolerable to discuss books with. I had forgotten to tell her to keep my secret, though, and I felt a moment of panic. Madam Hale obviously knew, as well as Gypsum, who had read my file, but it would be nice not to tell anyone else I was Solhan. Of course, Juliette would blab to all and sundry. Maybe there was no hope for it.

I sighed and decided to find out which class I was missing. I could always plead first day ignorance. On the way out, I was blocked by a teacher with ochre eyes. Not as interesting eyes as most dwarf females, which made their dullness noteworthy. Her gaze bore into the book I carried.

"Did you check that out, young lady?"

I couldn't even remember which one I'd grabbed and read the spine, A History of Weaving in the Dwarvish Highlands, and shuddered. "No." I placed it on the nearest shelf.

She appraised me like a slave buyer assessing the wares, noticing the bad dye job and looking at my eyes a lot. I had faith in the charm that made them blue. Nanny had refused to craft one for me, calling it deceitful and elvish, which I kind of agreed with, but I also hated being instantly marked for a Solhan everywhere I went. So, I'd saved up my allowance, a year's worth, and bought it. The charm was stitched into a kerchief I carried. Duane had offered to steal me one, but it was best not to anger those who dealt in magic. I knew it was a good quality one, and the teacher couldn't see through it.

Finally, her assessment of my limited worth complete, she said, "I'd stay away from that girl. Solhan madness is catching."

"No, it's not," I shot back.

From her frown, I realized I'd forgotten the first rule of finishing school: don't speak unless spoken to. Actually, just don't speak.

"You're too young to have a free period, one of the new crop just arrived I wager," her tone carefully building to something I sensed I would not like, "What's your name?"

"Karolyne," I lied. I hoped this wouldn't be a permanent blot on Karo's record; she'd hate that, but I couldn't stop myself. I badly wanted to wriggle out of the dwarf's stare. I sensed she was hunting for the new Solhan to harass. Why else was she studying my disguise so intently? Pretending to be Karo didn't make any difference, though.

"You have detention. Come this way."

I followed, head down. Who got detention for skipping class to go to the library? This was the worst place in the world Uncle could have sent me, and now I knew why he'd done it. He was torturing me like Ilsa tortured mice, only he didn't care enough to come watch. Simply knowing I was in misery must be enough for him.

The teacher brought me to a full classroom and presented me to a younger dwarf woman I hadn't met before. "Miss Halcyon, this human is truant from her class this period. I will leave her with you. As Schedule Mistress, you can sort out where she should be. Make sure you also schedule in detention with me at the end of the day."

"Yes, Madam Jaspar, as you wish. However, I do have a class now, as you can see."

"Put this one into the queue with the others. I'm sure one more to check for posture won't be too taxing on a young and energetic instructor such as yourself," the ochre-eyed Madam Jaspar said, before departing.

When she was gone, Miss Halcyon and I both scowled at her retreating back.

"It's Lady Halcyon, not Miss, by the way," she told me.

"What class does Madam Jaspar teach that's so important?"

"It's her seniority that makes her important. Come along now, Miss...?"

"Thorne." No reason to get Karo into trouble now.

I'd have double detention when I admitted the lie to Madam Jaspar later. I was already having double deportment lessons. Wonderful.

# 3  TROUBLE

Gypsum didn't find me until the end of the day, when I was lounging on my bed studying the detention note Miss Halcyon had given me. The tower office. Where was that? When I asked Gypsum, Karolyne took the note and read it aloud. They both looked disappointed to hear I'd gotten myself into trouble.

"Going to the library." I rolled my eyes, emphasizing the absurdity of it all, but it wasn't penetrating their disapproving expressions.

"You'll be in worse trouble if you stay here," Karolyne said. "It doesn't help anyone, me included, for you to be on the teachers' radar. Keep your head down next time." She sounded like Morgan.

"I'll show you the way." Gypsum stood by the door, and I knew I was being forced to do the right thing. Follow the rules, anyway, which I didn't always think was the right thing.

"Fine." I stuck my tongue out at Karo before I followed the muddy-colored dwarf.

She led me a winding path, down and then up the stairs, and I'd never find my way back. I wasn't sure that was a bad thing. I could hide until the semester was over.

"Madam Jaspar's office." Gypsum indicated the door in front of us. She shook her head. "She's one step below the Headmistress and not an enemy you want to have. Do everything she asks, and be polite about it, and you may be okay."

"What will I have to do?" My imagination had assumed detention meant I'd be put in the stocks or something. I hadn't expected to do anything.

"Grade papers, sharpen charcoals, that sort of thing. She teaches geography but is a cartographer in her own time, a brilliant artist who has captured the tiniest bends in the Serpent's Ribbon. Her work is referred to by the Crowns themselves. You'd do well to learn anything you can from her."

"I'm not good at drawing."

"What are you good at?"

"Not much of anything. Although...Morgan says I have a knack for swordplay."

"I'll try to get you into fencing then. I'll try, so be nice here—and everywhere. Madam Jaspar knows far-seeing magic; it's what lends her work such accuracy. She can see what you're up to no matter where you are."

"A fiendish skill for a teacher to have. Can she hear me too?"

"I'm not sure." Gypsum suddenly looking a bit panicked herself. So, she wasn't always Miss Perfect.

"Let's hope not, or she really won't like me much, because I have a hard time keeping my mouth shut." I steeled myself and knocked.

Gypsum darted off, afraid to be spotted with me when the door opened. Only it didn't open. I knocked a couple more times, but there was no reply. I leaned against the doorjamb then, a terrible example of deportment I knew, and waited.

I had to shift positions a few times to stay comfortable, and I didn't know how much time passed, but it was a while, before I finally gave up. If Madam Jaspar had forgotten about my detention, I wasn't going to remind her. In fact, I'd call all this waiting around time served. I nodded to myself, firmly convinced by that argument, and headed back to my room. Karo was already asleep, so I climbed into my bed and let her snores lull me to sleep too. Nanny's snores were far worse, shaking the whole house, so I didn't mind.

I did mind, however, being awoken in the middle of the night. I'd been having a wonderful dream, only I couldn't remember what it was. There had been a waft of cinnamon, like something yummy cooking. I loved that smell. Nanny had never cooked anything edible in my life. Perhaps my mother had baked? I liked to think that was where the memory came from.

I couldn't figure out what had disturbed me. Karo was still snoring away, the room dark and quiet. Solhan eyes saw well in the dark. Nothing there. I shifted, and something clattered to the ground. I jumped to my feet, ready to fight. Then I noticed a necklace lying on the ground. It must have fallen off my bedclothes. That gave me a chill, thinking someone had crept in and placed it there.

I examined the deep green jewel in a silver setting. The setting resembled a gear from a clock or other contraption I usually paid little attention to. The chain was silver as well, which was odd to me for some reason, but then I remembered that dwarves never wore silver. The mines of their kingdom produced gold and precious gems beyond imagining, but no silver, and so it was traditional to avoid the metal to avoid ill luck. It must belong to one of the other students.

I immediately thought of Juliette. Was she clumsily trying to curse me? If so I should tell her it was only a dwarf thing.

In the morning, I'd tell her.

I was tired.

I opened my trunk to place the necklace inside and was captivated for a moment by the deep green stone. I couldn't figure out what it was, for it wasn't jade. It had an inner glow that, for some reason, made me think of my cinnamon dream. I'd seen plenty of precious gems cross my uncle's desk, so this one must be worthless, if pretty. I laid it gently inside and then laid my head back on the pillow. I fell asleep in an instant.

The next day, I decided to do some investigating to see who had been sneaking around in my room. Karo was my first point of call.

"I didn't hear a thing. I also haven't been here long enough to make enemies, so it must be your enemy. You make them quickly."

I smirked. "I figured that."

My first class was cooking. I was to make my own breakfast. Not a good idea. My porridge burned and stuck to the bottom of the pan in minutes, probably because instead of stirring it, I was listening to the whispers carrying across the classroom like an excited breeze through a forest of saplings.

"What is it?" I asked the dwarf girl nearest me. I was the only human in the class, so I'd been excluded from the gossip and hadn't been able to make out what they were saying.

The dwarf had yellowish skin and topaz eyes, the overall effect being the appearance of extreme jaundice.

She eyed me warily, like I was dangerous. "Someone attacked Madam Jaspar last night."

"Really?" That explained why she hadn't met me for detention. I didn't say that part out loud. "Do you know when it happened?"

"Aren't you going to ask if she's all right?"

"Of course I was. Is she?"

"She's in the infirmary."

I nodded and went back to scraping my porridge pan, calmly trying to dislodge the burnt chunks, while my thoughts churned.

Had a thief been prowling the grounds last night? I shivered, thinking he might have been in my room and inadvertently left some of his treasure behind. But that didn't explain whose necklace it was, nor why Madam Jaspar of all people had been attacked. Maybe she'd seen the thief? This wasn't Highcrowne, else I'd worry it was someone I knew. I was curious to learn who the culprit was. No dwarf would steal what they saw as a cursed necklace. Unless they only spotted its nature later and tossed it on my bed on their way out? There was a window at the end of the hall near my room.

As soon as class was over, I darted out, but I ran into Lady Halcyon going the other way.

"Slow down," she ordered. "No running in the halls. Wait. Eva, is it?"

"Yes."

"You had detention scheduled with Madam Jaspar last night."

"She didn't show, I swear." I knew I sounded guilty, but I couldn't help myself. "I waited and waited...."

"Child, you should know the Madam was attacked." She paused, as though expecting it to be news to me, so I went along.

"No! By who? How?"

"By whom. We do not know any particulars, for she is still resting. The faculty is asking all the girls to be wary and report any strangers sighted on the grounds."

"Yes, Miss...Lady Halcyon." I curtsied, poorly, as I hadn't had that class yet, but I was dismissed and able to continue on my way. I headed for the infirmary.

The nurse wasn't in sight, and there was only one patient in the beds, so I went straight to Madam Jaspar's side. She was asleep. I noted the scratches on her face and arms. Whoever she'd fought must have been part feral cat.

There was a large bandage around her abdomen, and I lifted the corner, trying to peek inside. A hand slapped down on mine, and I jumped back with a start.

Madam Jaspar's dull, ochre eyes were open and glaring at me.

"I was only curious," I said. "Are you alright? What happened?"

She tried to speak but nothing came out. I handed her a glass of water from the bedside table, and she wetted her lips. "Don't think I've forgotten your detention."

"Shouldn't we all focus on finding your attacker? What if he strikes again?"

"There is little chance of that."

"What makes you so certain?" I began, feeling a torrent of unanswered questions ready to pour out of my mouth, but the nurse returned.

"Get away now. Your Solhan filth could infect the wound." The nurse shooed me.

She must have read my file. No escaping records and paperwork, despite what enchantments I wore or what color my hair.

People believed Solhans were plague carriers. With some justification, but the plague that affected humans affected us as well. Dwarves were immune, though, so they had nothing to worry about.

I backed away. "How was she wounded?"

"She was stabbed," the nurse said accusingly. "Go and fetch one of the teachers.

I nodded and took one last look at Madam Jaspar. That look chilled me. She'd heard me called a Solhan, and now she knew too. Her expression was a mixture of disgust and fury. I wasn't welcome here, so I darted out and found Madam Hale. She grabbed others and hurried to the infirmary, while I returned to my room and sat glumly on the edge of my bed.

I don't know how many classes I missed that morning. I was dazed, and time passed strangely. It had been a mistake to come here. Gernwold had more Solhan-haters than Highcrowne. They wouldn't take in human refugees, so they probably didn't enjoy people like Karo around either. What had Uncle been thinking? He should have left me alone, where I was happy.

Gypsum found me later and removed the pillow from my face. "What are you doing here? I thought you wanted to study fencing? I had it added to your schedule."

I hadn't looked at my schedule since breakfast. I had noted the fresh sheet of paper hung by my door but ignored it.

"What's the point? I'm going home first chance I get." Uncle wouldn't like that, but he didn't need to know. I could live on the streets, like Duane. Of course, Duane wouldn't want me around either. I had no place, nothing.

"You're experiencing boarding school blues is all. Happens all the time around here. It doesn't help that you missed the orientation and introduction party. Half the girls in this school don't know each other and are as vulnerable and scared as you. But you have even less reason to be than most! There's Karolyne, and me. I want to be your friend."

"How could you? I'm Solhan. Perhaps you're only fascinated by the freak." I was reminded of my conversation with Hazel. She had boarding school blues too.

"Never ever say that. The Solhans are a great people, a heritage you should be proud of."

"You've never met a Solhan before have you?"

"Well, no."

"Few are 'great'. More like 'irate', 'angry' and just plain 'cruel'. Best you avoid being my friend."

"I'll be the judge of who is good and who is cruel, and I haven't seen anything deplorable about you. A bit of sloth, but nothing a good schedule can't over-come."

I cringed at the word 'schedule', and her expression softened.

"But, it's my solemn duty to make up for your missing the arrival party. How about we both skip out this afternoon and I take you into town? Cakes, pastries, tea in the ice gardens, window shopping.... You'll like it."

"Ice gardens?"

"Of course. Gernwold is cold. But the tea is hot."

Cakes too. My stomach rumbled. "That sounds better than whatever else was on my schedule for this afternoon."

"Let's go." Gypsum took my arm, but her grip was broken when Karolyne raced between us and began tearing through her trunk.

"Hey!" I said. "What's up?"

"Madam Jaspar is awake." Karolyne was frightened.

"I know."

"And she says a student attacked her, one with a cursed silver necklace. They're searching everywhere for it and the culprit!"

"Crap." I started tearing through my own trunk.

"What's going on here?" Gypsum asked.

Karo emerged with a bottle of gin. "Hiding contraband. The school guards are searching every room. Where am I going to put this?"

Gypsum had a sour, disappointed expression, but a moment later it softened and she sighed. "I know a place. Come on."

I tucked the necklace in the pocket of my school jacket and turned to follow.

"What do you need to hide?" she asked.

"I forgot. I don't have contraband now, but I'm likely to later. So, show me where to hide it when I get it."

"You are strange," Gypsum mumbled.

The three of us slunk out the door and around the corner. I heard boots echoing down the hallway, followed by the wooden sounds of overturned drawers and chests. "They're close by."

"It's not far," Gypsum reassured me.

Soon we were in a deep alcove, hiding behind an urn that stood on a marble pedestal.

"Where to now?" Karo asked. The footsteps were headed our way.

"We're here." Gypsum clambered atop the pedestal and lifted the lid of the urn. It made the *sculp* sound of fine china pieces scraping together. "Put it inside."

"This hidey hole is not big enough to stash a body," I pointed out.

Gypsum froze.

"She's kidding," Karolyne said. "It's a Solhan thing."

I nodded. At least I thought I was kidding. Sometimes I didn't know myself.

Karo was taller than Gypsum and had no difficulty reaching inside to set the bottle of gin gently on the bottom. "This isn't going to work. They'll look here."

"As long as it's not in your possession, what's the matter?" Gypsum asked.

"I might want the gin back when winter sets in. Something to keep the chill away."

"Then move it again later when the coast is clear. We must go now." She ushered us off. They were ransacking our room now, only a few doors down.

Karolyne and Gypsum headed the opposite way, but they turned back when they saw I wasn't following. "Come on."

"Let's split up," I said. "Meet you at supper."

Gypsum pulled Karo's arm, shaking her head, and the two of them soon vanished into the depths of the school.

I climbed atop the pedestal and dropped the necklace inside. I nearly dropped the ceramic lid too, when a voice behind me said, "You can't leave it there."

It was Hazel. She was hiding in the shadows, and I hadn't heard her sneak up behind me.

"Hiding some of your own contraband?" I asked. Hazel didn't seem the type to break the rules. Then again, she was half-Solhan.

"You can't let Madam Jaspar get hold of it."

"Why not?"

"You can't...."

There was no time to argue with her or hide it anyplace else, because one of the guards was coming right for us. I stepped boldly into the corridor and started walking.

"You there," he said, and I stopped. "Turn out your pockets."

I turned and did as he asked, glad my jacket was empty now. There were no pockets in my dress, but he eyed my boots and stockings, as though I might hide something in there. I took them off and threw them at him. "Is this how ladies are treated in Gernwold?"

"Apologies." He was a reddish dwarf who grew redder looking at my bare ankles. I lifted my skirt, about to show him there was nothing in my garter either, but he held up a hand. "There's no need for that, young lady. My mother would whip me for being so disrespectful to a lady, even a human."

I would have felt some sympathy for his predicament if he hadn't added 'even a human'. As it was, I pounced on his hesitation. "I bet you enjoy this chance to ogle school girls. What sort of a man searches through our private things, unless he takes some pleasure in it?"

My words and brazen pose were making him un-comfortable. He looked at the ground and pulled at the ruffled collar that hung over the rim of his etched breastplate. He said, "Only following orders."

"Now that is the worst excuse, and yet I hear it every day. Whenever a new band of refugees arrives in Highcrowne, city guards, 'following orders', send the women and children into the slums and the men are paraded before the shipmasters who draft whoever they like into interminable 'employment', sometimes never to be seen again. Those are the lucky ones. My uncle's minions 'follow orders' whenever they offer food in exchange for muscle, for gangs of desperate men to war with other desperate gangs. Victim or tyrant, all claim to be following orders of man or gods and take no responsibility for themselves. Are you another tyrant? Another victim?"

The guard seemed thoroughly off kilter from my lecture, his mouth open, speechless. His compatriot showed then to ask what was happening, and the guard dragged him away from me, clearly eager to avoid any further moral contemplation.

"Hmm." I smirked at their departing backs.

I put my boots and stockings back on and looked around for Hazel, but she was nowhere to be found. She was a sneaky one.

I left the necklace where it was, now that I had managed to divert the search from this area. I'd come back for it tonight and find a better hiding place.

Maybe in the meantime, someone would tell me what was so special about it.

# 4  Found Out

Classes that afternoon were awash in whispers. I missed Fencing and was stuck with Knitting and Rhetoric. Rhetoric might have been interesting, if the instructor had wanted to discuss current issues and hadn't, instead, been reviewing tired arguments for the matriarchy that were centuries old. Gypsum was in all my classes, so I knew she'd pulled strings to be there. She wanted to ask what I'd been up to, I could tell, but there was no opportunity with every whisper squashed by watchful teachers. Gypsum and I never did sneak out for some time on the town because the gates were locked.

They were locked the next day too, and the one after that. Gypsum forgot to ask me anything, and I forgot to move the necklace. It hadn't been found, and I didn't have any place better to hide it.

At dinner, on the third day after all the excitement, Madam Hale led prayers to the dwarven gods of hearth, home and education. Madam Jaspar was there, and she stood to speak too. She was pale and trembled, the bandage around her midriff plain for all to see. Why hadn't they paid a mage to heal her? I would have thought a fancy school like this would take care of its own. Many of the other teachers attempted to offer a helping hand, but she waved them off.

Karolyne sat beside me and Gypsum across from me. One nudged me in the ribs and the other kicked my shin to make sure I was paying attention, but I already was. I was hanging on every facial expression to see who she would accuse as her attacker. Would it be a Solhan?

I hadn't spotted Hazel lately and wondered if she was in hiding. Someone had told me she'd gone home, but I didn't believe that for a second. Her home was worse than mine, her birthright a taint. That kind of thing could weigh on a person, make them depressed or angry. I knew from experience, and I usually went for angry. Had Hazel done something? Had she attacked the teacher?

Or would Madam Jaspar blame me, knowing full well I was innocent, if only to expunge a filthy Solhan from her presence?

Madam Jaspar looked at no one as she spoke, her gaze distant. "I have only recently recovered from a fever that set in from my wound. Many of you may know I blamed a student for the attack, but it was a fever dream. My...apologies." The word seemed difficult for her to utter. "I'm unsure who attacked me. A thief perhaps. Nevertheless, I am looking for a necklace that was stolen from me. It is silver, featuring a rare variety of green jasper, and is a dear family heirloom. The thief may have absconded with it, but if anyone has knowledge of its whereabouts or how to find it, I will provide a generous reward." She sat back down again, and quiet reigned.

I didn't think anyone had expected her to claim the cursed necklace or show such single-minded concern for it.

Finally, Madam Hale stood again. "Thank you for your apology, Madam Jaspar, but no one blames you for your fever. We all wish we could do more to find justice for you. The guard on the school has been doubled, to protect from future incursions, and we will do all we can to find this heirloom. It must be precious indeed." She didn't add 'for you to bear it being silver' but we heard the unspoken sentiment.

I was quiet too, and bemused. Karolyne and I returned to our room. Gypsum came along with us, wildly conjecturing. "Perhaps she's a sorceress?"

"Madam Jaspar? Why?" I asked.

"Farseeing? Silver?" Gypsum made it sound like those were obvious signs.

"Why can't she far-see where the necklace is?" Karo wondered, logical as always.

"What difference does it make if she's a sorceress, witch, mage, enchanter or whatever you want to call her?" I said.

It wasn't illegal to practice magic in the Kingdoms, even for pay, and a title was only used if you were a professional in your craft. Many people dealt in weak spells, amateurs, while those of great skill were usually involved in the war effort. If they were human that was. The mysterious Avians, who ruled the Kingdoms alongside the Matriarchs and Elf King, did not concern themselves with external matters, and they were as magical as it was possible to be. Elven magic was pervasive too, almost all elves had it, but it wasn't powerful. There were very few magical dwarves. Maybe that's why Madam Jaspar was of note?

"If she's a sorceress, perhaps the necklace is necessary for her spells? It could be what gives her that legendary far-seeing ability? That would explain why she needs it so badly. How will she make maps without it?" Gypsum seemed smug about her reasoning.

"That does make sense," I admitted.

"Yes," Karo agreed. "Do you think they'll search our rooms again?"

"It sounds like she is relying on someone wanting the reward to find it now," Gypsum said. "But, you never know. It would be a good excuse to ferret out any more contraband. I hear Juliette had a flask of whisky in her bag. She's a month detention to look forward to. What is it with you human girls and drink? We dwarves are raised on barley ale; it's a food-stuff and the easiest way to import barley, as mice are unlikely to eat it fermented. Why the need for hard liquor?"

"Because our parents would be furious," Karolyne said. "Why else? Plus, you can't get as drunk on barley ale. It fills you up before you go blind. We need something to help the school years blur by."

"Maybe I should have brought some too," I mused, not that I thought numbing my brain was the best way to rebel against my family. Using my brain was probably the best revenge.

"Never fear." Karolyne removed the candlesticks from a side table. She pulled off the tablecloth, and then I saw it wasn't a side table at all. Actually, it hadn't been there this morning. It was a crate. "I have enough to keep everyone well lubricated. Mail arrived today with my shipment. I have a consignment deal with a Highcrowne distillery who were willing to back me, knowing I could operate inside the school. Only, that urn isn't big enough to hold all this. I need you to help me bury it in the woods. Someplace I can hide this long term. There's a forest at the edge of the grounds; I checked."

"Oh my gods," Gypsum exclaimed. "A bottle of gin is one thing, but a bootleg conspiracy? Who are you people?"

"Descendants of merchants," Karolyne said.

"Criminals in my case," I said. "At best."

"I suppose that explains it." Gypsum's look of shock slowly transformed into one of mischief. "You two are way more fun than anyone else in this school."

"The guard has been doubled," I reminded Karo. "Madam Hale said so. How are we to get your stash to safety?"

We both looked at Gypsum, and she shrugged. "I'm out of ideas."

"The window at the end of the hall," I said. "I hang around down on the ground to collect each basket of booze, while one of you lowers it down a few at a time and the other runs lookout."

"I'll run lookout below with you, Eva," Gypsum said.

"You're volunteering?" Karo asked, surprised. "On the ground is probably the riskiest job, because of the patrols."

"I'm far better at talking my way out of trouble than either of you, besides it sounds fun." Gypsum was taking quickly to our bootleg conspiracy.

"We can't let you do that," I said. "You're an innocent, and it's bad enough we're corrupting you.

We can't let you get caught. Karolyne, you're on the ground with me. Gypsum runs lookout up above while we get...Juliette to lower the bottles." I was amazed by the words coming out of my mouth. "She's already got detention, so what does she have to lose?"

I had thought about Hazel first, but she was nowhere to be found. I wanted to know what she knew, anyway, so if I found her I wouldn't waste breath on this silly scheme. I'd hit her with some real questions instead.

"More months of detention," Karolyne pointed out. "I thought you hated Juliette. Or is this part of the plan? Get her in worse trouble?"

"I do sort of hate her, but we need help. Gypsum and she have nothing against each other. Right?"

Gypsum nodded. "You humans all look alike."

"Funny," I said, thinking humans believed the same about dwarves. "Give her some whisky in payment, Karo. You do have whisky in there?"

"I do. Fine. It's a plan." Karo made us all swear a blood oath not to betray one another. That meant sharing a few drops of pinky blood, released using our embroidery needles and mixed in a thimble before we each downed a sip. It wasn't a real Solhan blood ritual, so I thought nothing of it. Nobody died and no souls were bound. They took it seriously though.

"If we get Juliette to swear too, I'll be happy," Karolyne said.

We hung back as Gypsum approached Juliette. The blonde girl was sitting by herself in the common room. Seemed she didn't have any friends either, at least the other human girls weren't with her, and the dwarves avoided her as much as they did us Solhans. We all looked alike after all.

"Juliette, is it?" I heard Gypsum say.

I ducked out of sight before she could see I was involved. She'd refuse outright if she caught sight of me and Karolyne. This all had to be Gypsum's plan.

"Let's find a rope," I told Karolyne. "A basket too. Something to lower things down."

"The well!" she and I said at the same time. It's like we should have been twins. Maybe the red hair had put us in synch?

We hurried to the well house behind the kitchens. I had a sheathed knife in my garter, so it was good the guardsman hadn't let me show more leg the night before. I would have been punished worse than detention for that, even expelled, but that suited me fine. I'd definitely need the dagger if I was living on the streets. I used it to cut the rope, while Karolyne made sure no one from the kitchen came in and caught us vandalizing things.

I hid the knife again and rolled the rope up so it was inside the bucket. I tossed in some potatoes from the cold storage in the well house, and then whistled as I strolled back inside and up to our room. It was nearly dark and time for curfew.

Juliette was there, a smear of blood on her lips.

"You took the oath?" Karolyne was serious.

"I swore to Gypsum. She promised me a winter's supply of whisky," Juliette said.

Karolyne glared at Gypsum, but nodded. "More than the bottle I had in mind, but fine. As long as you agree to help with future shipments, you're in."

Juliette's expression soured. "This once."

"A winter's supply is two bottles then."

"Fine."

"Done." Karolyne spat in her hand, but Juliette refused to shake.

"Disgusting," the new member of the pact said. "Hand over the bucket and let's be done with this."

I held on to it. "You need to go back to your room for lights out. Return at midnight. We make our move in the witching hour." I used my ominous voice, but I didn't look as Solhan as I should, so the effect failed.

Juliette flipped her hair and strutted out. Gypsum followed, saying, "See you soon."

I didn't sleep a wink, fretting over what could go wrong. I listened to the footsteps of the guards, taking note of their route and timings. They flashed a lantern in our room every hour, which meant we had an hour to transfer the stash between patrols.

When the other girls showed, I jumped out of bed, fully dressed and ready to go. Gypsum smothered a yelp, while Juliette stayed quietly determined not to acknowledge my existence. We had to wake Karolyne up.

"This is all for you, you know. The least you can do is be alert," I told her.

Karolyne rubbed her eyes. "Sorry. I'm awake."

I slapped her once to make sure, and from her gasp and the glare she gave me, I knew that had done the trick. While Gypsum and Juliette loaded some pillow-cases with the bootleg hooch, Karo and I took the well bucket to the window and tied the rope to the marble plinth the urn rested on.

I told Karo I'd fetch her gin, and I grabbed the necklace when I did. I got a flash of Hazel's white eyes, remembering when she snuck up on me before. I checked the shadows but there was no one there now.

Karolyne was leaning out the window. "I don't think we thought out this bit of the plan. Let's go through the kitchen."

"We have no idea when the patrols run down there. Come on, we're only two stories up." I climbed out the window, holding to the rope as I braced my feet and walked my way down.

I'd done this kind of thing plenty of times when helping Duane and Viktor. Okay, well maybe not a lot of it myself, but I'd seen it done. Two stories was higher than it sounded, though, and I fought a wave of vertigo.

Despite hours drying in my room, the bottom portion of the rope was slimy with algae. I shuddered to think we were drinking that stuff. The school should check the well quality. I blamed the algae for my slip, although it was likely the vertigo.

I lost my footing along with my grip and plummeted face first. Ancient hedges saved me, for they were thick with evergreen needles and springy branches to break my fall. Of course, they broke the skin as well, and I bled from a dozen scratches. My uniform jacket was torn in places, and I felt the sting of open air on a bigger gash beside my knee. I moaned and rolled out of the bushes, grateful for the thin layer of snow that caught me, the cold dulling some of the throbbing pain.

Karolyne learned from my mistake and wrapped the rope around her forearm as she descended. She had a few wobbles, but she made it down behind the hedge rather than inside it. She got a few scratches clearing a path to me, but the path she took wasn't too over-grown. Others had come this way before, and possibly the thief who stabbed Madam Jaspar.

"Are you alright?" Karolyne hovered over me.

"Yes. Feeling stupid, though. Can you help me up?" When I was on my feet, I wobbled but remained stand-ing. I was going back through the kitchen this time, even if I got caught.

Juliette hauled the bucket up and then lowered the first batch. I was supposed to be emptying the bucket, but I was staying away from the hedge that had attacked me, so Karolyne and I switched jobs.

I was on lookout and spotted a couple of noisy guards chatting their way around the perimeter. They weren't very good at guarding, which explained the intrusion the other night. We had plenty of time to hide the rope and duck out of sight. I went into the woods a bit, where I had a clearer view of their route, and gave the all clear when they were gone. I reckoned we had about half an hour left before a patrol returned to our rooms upstairs.

Juliette lowered the remaining bottles and Gypsum waved goodbye out the window. Their job was done, but ours was only beginning. We carted four, heavy pillowcases between us, the bottles clinking together.

The woods were dark, and Karolyne couldn't see a thing, so I guided her. She cursed and stumbled every few feet. The school was at the edge of the city, the forest cultivated, not wild; I could tell by the even rows. In the centuries since it was planted, however, the trunks had grown huge and undergrowth had taken over, so it might as well have been a dense forest in the depths of the mountains. I took us on a straight path from the window we'd descended from, so we'd be able to find the stash again later.

I'd forgotten to bring a shovel, of course. I used my dagger to cut up some of the frozen sod, but it wasn't going very deep. I gave up after a few tries. "Looks like we'll need to cover the sacks with some tree limbs. You stay here while I find some."

"By myself?" Karolyne's voice shook. It was almost pitch black. Almost, as I had enough moonlight filtering through the branches to see, but situations like this made it obvious Solhans weren't humans. Karolyne couldn't even tell where I was standing; she kept looking around, her gaze unfocused. I turned her shoulders and pointed her in the direction of the school.

"Why don't you head back and watch for patrols?" I said. "This won't take me long."

"Good idea." If she didn't have to stumble and feel her way back, I knew she would have been running to reach the edge of the woods. She was that terrified.

I felt safer cloaked in darkness, so I shrugged and went looking for fallen branches. I found one that managed to mostly cover the bags, when Hazel found me.

"How...?" I began, but then I remembered she was Solhan too. This was like a midday stroll for us.

"Throw the necklace into the well," she said. "Do whatever you have to, but you need to get rid of it."

"How do you know I have it?" I couldn't help being coy, because I wanted to learn more. "What is so important about it, anyway?"

"I wouldn't be here if you didn't have it. It's in your pocket." As soon as she said it, I felt it grow warm and emit a green light that spilled through the weave of my jacket to illuminate the clearing around us.

"Oh no," Hazel said. "He is calling me. We're running out of time. Smash it..." She couldn't finish whatever else she wanted to say, because she was pulled
backwards into the woods by some invisible force. Her
arms reaching out to me in desperation.

I felt the necklace in my jacket being pulled too. It
was going to tear through my pocket. I grabbed hold
but wasn't strong enough to resist. I had to let go, or
it would go through me as easily as cloth. I held on
anyway and ran to keep up with Hazel, allowing the
force tugging at the gemstone to propel me.

We reached a small, stone building overgrown with
greenery. Only a peak of roof was visible and an open
doorway that glowed orange with firelight. An ornate,
iron gate blocked the path, but Hazel went right
through it. The gate didn't move, but she passed
through like mist.

I stopped and blinked. The necklace wanted to
follow, so I couldn't hold back for long. I hurried to the
gate and opened it, the metal hinges protesting with a
screech.

The building was plain stone on the outside, but
inside was all bronze and copper. The walls were covered in panels of it, and secured to them were gear
wheels and cogs, interlocked in complex patterns. They
covered everything, and I couldn't see what they were
supposed to be turning.

It looked exactly like the innards of a water clock
I'd once seen in Highcrowne, with channels for the

water to flow and turn the gears, but there was no water and no clock face for the mechanical gizmos to
power. The only thing I saw the mechanisms leading to
was a trapdoor in the center of the floor. The door was
a slab of green stone, jasper like the necklace, and bar-
ren of metal or gears. It did have one small slot for a
cog, which would connect it to the rest of the
mechanized room—a slot the perfect size for the necklace's setting. The necklace was pulling me to it.

"Don't," Hazel warned.

I didn't have much choice. The necklace slammed
against the stone, bruising my knuckles, and I let go. It
slid of its own accord, the silver gear fitting into its
slot perfectly.

The green gem glowed brightly then, lending its
glow to the slab of stone it rested in, and the cog
began to turn. It turned the silver gear and then the
bronze one nearest, gear after gear...until the entire
chamber was clattering. The squeak of disused metal
transformed into the groan of something shifting and
coming into mechanical life. The necklace was the
motor for all of it. And as my gaze followed the trail of
gears, it circled back to the central trapdoor, which
opened.

The sight of what was inside shocked me. I'd seen
dead bodies before, but never someone who was
murdered. There was blood everywhere in the small
chamber, splashed across the sides and pooled at the
bottom. It wasn't fresh, rather brown and old, but

nothing had been touched, and the body lay where it had fallen. It was Hazel.

I touched her. Her corpse was cold and hard as marble, pale skin ashen with all the blood drained from it.

"No," I said, the word heavy with shock.

Hazel was beside me, staring down at her own body. "Our god is calling me. It's time to rise again. I want to go to Him, but I can't. Destroy the necklace, Eva. Please."

Hazel was a ghost. I realized that now. She'd been dead for days, which meant our little chat in the library was probably the last time I'd seen her alive. Seemed I had inherited the Solhan curse of seeing things that weren't there, what others couldn't.

"You will not rise. Your soul is mine," a familiar voice said.

I turned and saw it was Madam Jaspar. She closed the chamber's gate with a screech.

"What...?" I began.

"Two Solhan souls now." The ochre-eyed teacher stalked toward me with a feral grin.

# 5   Time to Die

I fumbled with my dress and pulled the dagger from my garter. "Stay away from us." I waved it around, but I shook so much I knew I didn't look threatening at all.

"He's here," Hazel said.

I looked back and saw Hazel's body twitching. Closed eyes opened. Her milky, Solhan irises contrasting with black pupils that stared at a world beyond this one.

I felt a presence then—something familiar, dark and terrifying all at once. The corpse climbed out of the trapdoor, leaving blood behind that was now fresh and as semi-alive as her body. The red liquid flowed into drains and started spreading through the channels in the clockwork that I thought had been for water. Looked like blood worked as well.

The corpse's head turned toward me, mouth open as if to speak...then it burst into flame. Hazel's black hair went first, the flames spreading quickly and burning hot, and I had to back away from the inferno.

"Don't make me burn you as well," Madam Jaspar said.

She was right beside me, and I spun. She knocked the dagger out of my hand, her fist like a hammer, and the blade went flying, landing somewhere in the chamber with a clank of metal on metal.

The teacher threw down the fire charm she'd used to destroy Hazel's body and pulled her own dagger then. It was ceremonial, silver and etched with runes, but it looked sharp and effective enough. "I prefer to draw out your soul before you burn."

Now this was unfair. She was armed, and I wasn't. Evil teachers for you. They liked to have all the advantages. Usually, that meant textbooks with the answers in the back and years of repetitive knowledge, while you got ridiculed for not knowing something the first time you encountered it. This one, however, was evil in the literal sense: a necromancer, fueling her magic with the lives of her victims.

I had two things going for me, the first being Jaspar's wound. Hazel must have put up a real fight the other night and not died easily. I circled away, toward the teacher's bad side, and lashed out with a quick kick to the bandage.

Jaspar swiped with the blade and grazed my leg, but she doubled over from the pain of my blow, and I came down with my own fist to knock the dagger out of her hand. Only problem was, I wasn't as strong as her, and she held tight to the weapon.

I backed as far as I could across the room then. Hazel's ghost stood beside me and said, "You have to destroy the necklace. Set me free."

The second advantage I had was, I knew necromancers. I lived with a household full of them. Some people saw the glass half full, some half empty, while we Thornes ask, 'is there poison in that glass?'.

"What spell requires strong, Solhan souls?" I circled the room, keeping Hazel's body, now burnt to ash and charred bone, between us. "Surely not your far-sight? It's a cantrip, if I know anything about anything."

"I'm over four hundred years old." Even among dwarves, who lived to be two hundred, that was an achievement.

"I get it. Youth and beauty...except you skipped the beauty part."

"I long ago tired of waspish comments from children such as you. I look forward to cutting your tongue out before you die."

"Now, now," I said, "what would the Headmistress think if she heard you talking about students like that?"

"She'd probably agree you're all better off without tongues."

"So, she's part of your little cult too?" My gaze searched the mechanical chamber, but I couldn't spot anything I could pry free and use as a weapon.

"I dislike cults, and the Headmistress is no friend of mine," Jaspar said. "I find work such as this best done in secret. Only the dead know what I am, for you cannot trust the living."

The necklace that fueled this clattering room held Hazel's soul, I knew. When the rising corpse had called her ghost, it had called the necklace along with it. Now that the corpse, the vessel, was destroyed, the summons was weaker, but I still felt something. A force was beckoning Hazel to the Lands of the Dead.

"I don't think the dead like keeping your secrets," I said. "I don't think they like you very much at all."

"It doesn't matter. When I'm done, none of this will have happened."

"What are you babbling about?" I wanted to keep her talking as I searched, but part of me was genuinely curious. Villains always revealed their evil plans, at least in every story I'd ever read, and I hoped I'd get some answers.

"Turning back my own years? Staying young? That is nothing," Jaspar scoffed. "What if I could reset the world? Go back before you Solhans destroyed everything? Back before the Dead God came? I would kill every one of you if required."

This room...it was...? "This is a time machine?" I stared at the walls of the metal box containing us, its gears to nowhere churning away.

Maybe they weren't turning uselessly? Maybe they were churning up time, the world, or just us two inside? I had no idea how such a thing could work.

"And it is your destruction," Jaspar said.

It was madness. Impossible...And if it weren't?

I'd found my dagger, but instead of attacking with it, I stopped beside the silver cog that drove this miraculous engine. Could I trust the teacher? Was there a way to prevent everything? No war, no refugees, no Solhans or Thornes. No me?

Madam Jaspar's lips curled into a snarl when she saw me reaching for her coveted trinket, but too much distance, and Hazel's corpse, stood between us.

The necklace was a focus for all the souls Jaspar had harvested over the centuries, all for her own selfish reasons. A flask of lives that needed refilling from time to time and would need more fuel forever. And now she said she wanted to help the world?

She was no hero. She wanted to burn up Hazel's be-ing, use her up like a candle, sweet little Hazel who had never done anything to anyone. The necklace was not salvation: it was a prison. But not for much longer.

I slammed the hilt of my knife into the green stone in the center of the cog. There was a distinct cracking sound, like the ice covering a frozen lake shattering when too much weight was put on it. The gem's glow faded. The machine stopped turning.

More than Hazel's soul was released. There was a swarm of them, like fireflies. So many deaths. So many lost lives. It occurred to me I could catch them, but I wasn't sure how, or if I even should.

"No," Jaspar said, stunned.

I felt Hazel's ghostly lips touch my cheek then, not flesh but the memory of flesh, and she whispered, "Thank you, Eva. We choose who we are. We choose our future, not our past. I see that now. It doesn't matter whether we're born Solhan, human or elf; it's our choice. Or yours now. I have only one choice left, and I choose to go to Him. I will see you again. One day."

She was gone. I felt her passage, like a draft from an open door to somewhere I couldn't see, and an emptiness left behind.

"Now you've done it," Jaspar said. "I must start again. Craft a new cog, find new victims.... I have nothing with which to contain your soul now, so I must consume what I can. You don't get to linger as a ghost. You don't get any more time." She came at me with her ceremonial knife raised, ochre eyes hardened with fury.

I dove behind a now silent gear, causing Jaspar's first blow to skid across its bronze surface. She came at me with greater speed and fury the next time. I rolled but couldn't get far enough away, so I held up my dagger. It was impossible to block or parry her maniac charge, so I instinctively covered my face at the last moment, and her blade dug in.

I screamed as her knife went deep into my arm and shattered bone. She couldn't pull it out to strike again; it was stuck fast and getting slick with my blood. She cursed in frustration, and then she began an incantation. It was dwarvish. I'd studied languages at Morgan's knee ever since I could remember. The usage was archaic, yet I recognized enough words to know it was a spell to draw out my soul through the wound.

"From life to my life," Jaspar chanted, "from blood to my blood..."

She held the silver hilt steady, not that I could move my arm anyway. Any motion was agony. In a haze of pain, I tried to strike with my own weapon, but I was weak with shock, and she batted my effort aside, sending my dagger flying again. I gritted my teeth.

"...It's not working," she said in frustration. "Where is your soul?"

I didn't know what her problem was, but I relished the extra moments to think. Morgan played dirty in sparring practice and wasn't afraid to leave a bruise. He'd lectured me about ignoring pain. But this? Theory was different from practice, and a lot more painful.

I told myself this was the real thing. Anything goes. Better than to lose my life. I rolled, screaming as the knife in my arm shifted, but I kept rolling as far as I could, the dagger digging in more each time I struck the floor, but I didn't stop until I hit Hazel's burned remains and couldn't go any further.

I lay in the warm ashes suddenly thinking that would be me. I would be next to burn.

"By the Lightbringer! Eva!" It was Karolyne's voice, and instead of feeling relieved, I was suddenly more terrified. I couldn't let another friend die. I couldn't let Madam Jaspar win and keep on winning for more centuries to come.

"Get out of here. Find help!" I pulled a heat-cracked rib bone from the heap that had once been Hazel. I stood and faced Jaspar with the makeshift weapon, my back to the door, hoping Karo would listen to me and get out while she could.

Jaspar's eyes still glowed with fury. She was really upset that I'd broken her necklace and stopped her plan. I had mixed feelings about it myself, but I was certain I wanted to live.

"You want my soul? Come and get it." I beckoned.

She charged.

I raised the rib bone to block, but there was suddenly a sword there instead. The shining blade deflected the teacher's silver dagger and then swung around to rest on Jaspar's neck.

"Stop," the guard said. It was the one I'd made blush in the corridor the other night. "You are under arrest for murder and necromancy. By the laws of the Three Crowns, if you do not yield, I will kill you."

Jaspar snarled, and another guard came up behind her and struck the back of her head. She crumpled.

"Help her," Karo pleaded, and for a moment I thought she was talking about Jaspar. Then my friend wrapped her jacket around me and put her hand over the wound in my arm. The dagger was still stuck fast, but it had torn more flesh, and I realized I'd lost a lot of blood. A lot. A moment later I was on the floor too, and blackness swallowed my vision.

I woke in the infirmary, but I woke, which was the main thing. I was happy to be alive. The nurse, however, didn't look any happier to see me than the last time. At least she didn't kick me out. She checked my eyes and pulse and then my bandaged arm. There was some blood, but obviously not enough to induce her to change the dressing.

I had a few visitors over the following days. Guards, real city guardsmen, not school guards, asked me questions. I was too dazed about it all to lie, not that I was sure what I should lie about.

I didn't know how Jaspar's chamber of gears and cogs worked, or if it even did. She was a maniacal murderer, so she could be crazy. I think the guards thought so, because they didn't make many notes during that part of the story. They were more disturbed when I told them about seeing Hazel's ghost, and I wondered if that was a crime. Or was being Solhan enough to merit all the grilling?

In the end, no one arrested me, and I was released from the infirmary. Students whispered in the halls about Madam Jaspar. She was in prison. The whispers from some indicated she had done well to target Solhans, while others gave me more sympathetic looks. No one dared talk to me, only Karolyne and Gypsum, who hovered around me when I returned to my room, like it was another infirmary.

"They wouldn't let us in to see you," Gypsum said. "We were all questioned about Hazel and what happened. I can't believe it."

"I'm sorry I turned you in to the guards when I was caught," Karolyne told me. "I felt so guilty about it at the time, but it turned out for the best. If they hadn't made me help search for you.... We searched for hours."

"Hours?" It had felt like only a few minutes to me.

"What if we hadn't been there? There's no telling what could have happened," Karolyne continued.

"I would have died. That's what could have happened," I said.

They both quieted at that.

Death wasn't an unfamiliar sight in the Outskirts, but necromancy chilled everyone to the bone. It was forbidden, a tool of the great enemy.

Everyone knew Solhans had to be watched; if anyone was to break such laws it would be us. It surprised them a dwarf could be just as guilty of dark magic. Maybe that meant Solhans wouldn't automatically be suspected of every wrong doing? Maybe sentiments could one day turn to tolerance, or even something more? Understanding?

Maybe I was still light-headed from blood loss.

Karo and Gypsum respected my quiet attitude over the following months. I stopped dying my hair, and no one teased me about it. No one dared.

Eventually, the memories faded, and I laughed again.

We decided to hide our bootleg inventory in the old dungeon. It was safer than the woods and easier to get to. No ropes required. Juliette renewed her blood compact, with Gypsum anyway. She refused to mix with me, but we went back to blissfully ignoring one another's existence, even when working together.

I was glad when Karolyne gave up peddling hard liquor and instead got in on the latest fad of perfumed salts from Faellion. I felt better helping her sell that contraband.

Soon, summer came and with it our first visit home. I steeled myself before opening the coach door. The familiar scents and sounds of Highcrowne carried across the river. Not nice scents, but familiar ones.

I felt very different than I had when I'd left. I was a different person.

I swore I could hear Hazel's voice whisper against my skin again, telling me I could be who I wanted. I didn't forget it when I took my first step toward home. It was my choice who I'd be. And I knew I wouldn't be following orders.

## The End

If you enjoyed this young Eva tale, check out the new adult version of Eva Thorne in her epic, dark fantasy series full of mystery, with a touch of romance and more Steampunk flare!

TANGLE OF THORNES
A CROWN FOR A THORNE
BLOOD & THORNE
WAR OF THORNES (DECEMBER 2018)

# ABOUT THE AUTHORS

Lorel and Clayton were teen sweethearts. Clayton has severe dyslexia, but from the moment Lorel read 'Magician' aloud to him at age thirteen, they began to share magical worlds and dream of writing novels together one day. Hundreds of books later, and a wedding as well, those shared hours of reading, discussing and laughing, as they embellished their favorite stories, culminated in the completion of their first manuscript in 1996. After many more years of honing their craft, the Eva Thorne series was born. After the main four book series of Eva is complete, they are planning a new series of mysteries, as well as a science fiction series and a young adult fantasy. Stay tuned!

### CONNECT WITH LOREL CLAYTON

Website: www.lorelclayton.com
Twitter: @lorelclayton
Facebook: www.facebook.com/AuthorLorelClayton/
Instagram: www.instagram.com/lorelclayton/